Hairy Maclary Scattercat

Lynley Dodd

TRICYCLE PRESS

Berkeley, California

Hairy Maclary
felt bumptious and bustly,
bossy and bouncy
and frisky and hustly.
He wanted to run.
He wanted to race.
But the MAIN thing he wanted
was something
to
chase.

Greywacke Jones
was hunting a bee.

BUT ALONG CAME HAIRY MACLARY. . .

and chased her up high
in the sycamore tree.

Butterball Brown
was washing a paw.

BUT ALONG CAME HAIRY MACLARY. . .

and bustled him under
a rickety door.

Pimpernel Pugh
was patting a ball.

BUT ALONG CAME HAIRY MACLARY. . .

and chased her away
over Pemberton's wall.

Slinky Malinki
was down in the reeds.

BUT ALONG CAME HAIRY MACLARY. . .

and hustled him into
a drum full of weeds.

Mushroom Magee
was asleep on a ledge.

BUT ALONG CAME HAIRY MACLARY. . .

and chased her away
through a hole in the hedge.

Down on the path
by an old wooden rail,
twitching a bit,
was the tip of a tail.
With a bellicose bark
and a boisterous bounce,
Hairy Maclary
was ready
to
POUNCE.

BUT AROUND CAME SCARFACE CLAW...

who bothered
and bustled him,
rustled and hustled him,
raced him
and chased him…

ALL the way
home.

Other TRICYCLE PRESS books by Lynley Dodd
Hairy Maclary from Donaldson's Dairy
Hairy Maclary's Bone
Hairy Maclary's Rumpus at the Vet

☙

TRICYCLE PRESS
a little division of Ten Speed Press
P.O. Box 7123
Berkeley, California 94707
www.tenspeed.com

Library of Congress Cataloging-in-Publication Data
Dodd, Lynley.
Hairy Maclary scattercat / Lynley Dodd.
p. cm.
Summary: Hairy Maclary finds a variety of cats to chase, until
Scarface Claw bothers and bustles him, rustles and hustles
him, races and chases him all the way home.
ISBN 1-58246-095-7
[1. Dogs--Fiction. 2. Cats--Fiction. 3. Stories in rhyme.]
I. Title.
PZ8.3.D637Haj 2003
[E]--dc21

2002007703

First Tricycle Press printing, 2003
Manufactured in China

1 2 3 4 5 6 — 07 06 05 04 03